What is the M
Mrs Long?

written by Jay Dale
illustrated by Nick Diggory

"Oh, dear!" cried Mrs Long,
as she ran into Mr Lee's shop.

"Mrs Long," said Mr Lee.
"What is the matter?"

"Well!" said Mrs Long.

"I was walking down the street, when I saw a black and yellow tiger running in the park.

Then I saw a big green dinosaur
jumping up and down.
After that, I saw a little pink fairy
with a purple wand."

"Oh, dear!" cried Mr Lee.
"Are you ill?"

"Oh, yes!" said Mrs Long.
"I must be very ill."

"Mrs Long," said Mr Lee.

"Come with me.

I will take you to the doctor."

So Mr Lee and Mrs Long
walked out the door
and down the street.

All of a sudden,

they saw a black and yellow tiger

running in the park.

Then they saw a big green dinosaur

jumping up and down.

After that, they saw a little pink fairy

with a purple wand.

"Oh, dear!" said Mr Lee.
"I must be very ill, too!"

So they ran as fast as they could,
all the way to the doctor's house.

"Doctor! Doctor!" shouted Mr Lee.
"We were walking down the street,
when we saw
a black and yellow tiger
running in the park.
Then we saw a big green dinosaur
jumping up and down.
After that, we saw a little pink fairy
with a purple wand."

13

"Oh, dear!" said the doctor.

"You must be very, very ill."

Just then,

there was a knock at the door.

Rat-a-tat-tat! Rat-a-tat-tat!

"Come in," called the doctor.

In came a black and yellow tiger running this way and that.
Then came a big green dinosaur jumping up and down.
After that, came a little pink fairy with a purple wand.

"Trick or treat?" shouted the children.